Letters to Pauline

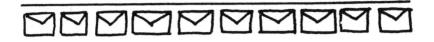

Letters to Pauline

James Krüss

translated by
Edelgard von Heydekampf Brühl
Atheneum 1971 New York

To all the friendly children
who wrote letters to me

Contents

Letters to Pauline

LETTER

1

THE AUTHOR TO THE READER

Something about Pauline,
trivial yet necessary details,
two houses and this book

Dear Reader,

This book contains an exchange of letters between my friend Pauline and myself. Therefore it is necessary that I introduce Pauline to you.

I have painted her picture here to show you what she looks like. I drew the picture from memory, because I have no photos of her. But I think the drawings do her justice. (Maybe even better than a photograph.)

I met Pauline when she had just started to go to school and was not yet able to read. (Therefore she was a very good storyteller.) She lives in a village near Munich where I lived at that time, too. Sometimes she would stop at my house on her way from school and tell me stories. These stories I bought from her for fruit, hard candy, chocolate, cold turkey, ice cream or nuts, and I made from them a book called Pauline and the Prince in the Wind. It is (if you want to call it that) the first book of Pauline. This book is then the second one. It varies in one important point from the first:

4

IN WINTER

IN SUMMER

PAULINE

IN SPRING

IN AUTUMN

MY HOUSE IN PAULINE'S VILLAGE

In this second book, I tell the stories.
For Pauline.

There are two reasons for this: First, Pauline
has learned by now to read and write. (Therefore she does not tell stories as prettily
as before.) Second, I don't live in Pauline's
village any more, but some thousand miles
away—on the Canary Islands, across from the
Sahara desert. And here there are some small
necessities that are hard to find, which
become dire necessities when you can't get
them. These small necessities were sent to me
by Pauline. In return I sent her letters,
stories, and pictures.

I'm showing you a picture of the house
where the first book took place. It is simple to
look at, and therefore simple to draw: my
house, the guest house, two small terraces,
and a tiny garden.

The house where I now live is impossible to
draw in a small space. Just for the main
house and terraces Number 1 and Number 3, I
need much more room than for both Bavarian

houses together. (Between the columns of the high terrace Number 1, you can actually see the windows of the guest house and a couple of the fieldstones of terrace Number 3.) In this Canarian house the second book started.

> I hope you like it!
> Your
> James Krüss

James Krüss

MY HOUSE

THE AUTHOR TO PAULINE

About being happy,
terraces, flowers, trees,
neighbors, St. Dolores,
hymns and address labels

Dear Pauline,

Thank you for your card asking whether or not I'm happy on my island. Frankly, I never know exactly when I am happy. Usually I only know it later, after the moment has passed, meaning afterwards. But if you mean to ask whether or not I like it here, let me assure you I like the sea and I like the island of Gran Canaria. Here, instead of the two terraces that I had in Germany, I have twenty-one terraces, even though some are no bigger than four towels laid end-to-end. I'll draw you a picture of Terrace No. 1. The container on the stone table is a Porron, a Spanish water pitcher from which one drinks by directing the water so it runs directly into one's mouth.

On my terraces, except for the two terraces on top of the roof (my terraces, you understand, are somewhat untidily stacked alongside a rock), there grow the flowers, bushes and trees of this area: Roses, Tan Trees (called here Gerbera), Mimosas, Calla, Gladiolas, Carnations, Hibiscus, Ivy, Passion flowers, Geraniums by the hundreds—red, pink and

12

white—and many kinds of Cacti. Among the different trees are lemon and orange trees, Indian laurel trees, Jacanda trees, which have blue blossoms, and the Aquate tree (a tree that bears a kind of vegetable), Magnolia trees (also called Tulip-trees) and some small Dragon's Worts, which nestle like turtles under other trees. For they grow almost as old as their namesakes: several hundred years, sometimes even several thousand years.

Just below my white-painted iron garden gate lives Manolito, the shepherd, with his family, and with sixty sheep and some goats, which he drives down into the gorge every morning and back again late at night. (The animals, not the family.) Behind my house live so many people that I still don't know all of them. They seem to be glued to the rock wall below my house in huts and very small houses. I only know old Juanita's family, where I buy eggs. Since yesterday, there are sixteen persons in her family, because Gloria, Juanita's daughter's daughter, had a little baby sister yesterday. And she, the new baby, can already cry.

Because my house has no windows in the back, I unfortunately have no view of this neighborhood. But during the next _fiesta_, when everyone stands on the top of his roof to watch the fireworks, I shall have an opportunity to count them. I guess there are seven families, because there are seven dogs.

Below my lowest terraces on the eastern side is a deep gorge. There I have only rats as neighbors. They never come to visit me because the rock is too steep.

Toward the South, behind a partly open white wall, is a rocky crag of bizarre volcanic stones, good only for growing fig cacti. Beyond this rocky crag is a semicircle of frizzed green and brown slopes, and in this valley a village called La Calzada.

La Calzada means—actually—a street. (The Spanish word calzada is road or route). The village has no church, no mayor and no policemen, but a bar, which serves very delicious rabbit with saffron and garlic, and a shop that looks like Ali Baba's hideaway. Only the treasures are not gold and precious stones, but sausages, hams, corn husks, bags of sugar, pots for cooking, light bulbs, straw baskets, woolen blankets, frankfurter sausages strung from a line, clusters of bananas and walls filled with wine bottles. This shop is also the post office.

Every afternoon at 4:10 sharp the bus from the capital of the island, Las Palmas, ar- rives with a mailbag. The mail-bus driver, Adolfo, who has a good sense of humor and flat feet, shuffles up to the counter with the bag, has the delivery paper signed, wishes everyone present much happiness and mail and drives on into the mountains. I wait for the mailbag to be emptied and pick out my mail from between the fresh sheep-cheese to my left and a bag of corn to my right. To me, Don Antonio, the shop's owner, seems to be a sort of Saint Nicholas, because he empties his bag for me each day on the counter. (You see from my drawing how it all happens.)

One is often reminded of saints on this island, because every village has a patron saint, and his name day is celebrated for an entire week with much noise, music and fireworks.

Our patroness is the Holy Mother herself, the Mother Dolorosa, whom we call Santa Dolores. Last week, we celebrated in her honor. (Here we call it a fiesta.) Seven fog horns boomed for seven days. Since the bar has only a few records, and at fiesta time it plays them loud, I learned them all by heart during the seven days. They are: "Kiss me, Kiss me . . . ," "La Paloma," "I love you" and "Poor, poor Bridegroom, oh poor Raphael."

For the name day of the patroness, I was invited by Don Antonio to a fabulous meal. We sat in his yard under a grape arbor and shared his chicken soup, fish, a side of beef, enormous platters of salad and very sweet cakes.

In the evening, a stall that sold sausages was put up in the village, and then came the smallest circus on earth. It performed on two kitchen tables brought out and pushed to-gether. There was something for everyone, but

it all came in small portions—a bit of everything to satisfy a large number of people: a
bit of dancing, a bit of singing, some acro-
batics, a bit of modest magic and the tiniest
clown in the world, as you will see from my
drawing, labeled with all the proper measure-
ments.

The Circus was followed by a "Procession
of Lights." Those in the procession carried
candles, using an upside-down bottle, from
which the bottom had been broken, as a candle
holder. The people sang very holy songs. But
the singers at the end of the procession
always remained one beat behind those who sang
in the front. In spite of it all, it was
very dignified.

That night I stood with a visitor from
Germany on the highest terrace of my house and
watched the fireworks. They shot like a
cannonball up into the sky, and burst in a
cascading rain of sparks, which came slowly
down, bathing all the surrounding mountains
in light.

After the show we heard fat Marero, the

THE TINIEST CLOWN
IN THE WORLD

MAIL

THE GRAN CANARIA POST OFFICE

"Rabbit keeper," asking through his bullhorn what the fireworks might have cost.

"One thousand Pesetas?" someone asked.

"More!"

"Two thousand?"

"More!"

"Four thousand?"

"Still more!"

"Seven thousand?"

"Yes, sir! Seven thousand pesatas!" Which is, after all, over one hundred dollars! I had given some money for those fireworks. At least one of the light cascades had been my contribution.

Can you find the name day of the Mother Dolorosa in your Calendar of Saints? Because I never heard of such a day in Germany.

Write to me about it; and send me, when you can, some gummed address labels like the ones they sell in the post office. Those for sale here are too small. Besides they have an ornate blue border that I don't like. I'll give you the money for them on my next trip to Germany.

This has been a long answer to a short

postcard. Maybe I'll get a long answering letter from you?

Regards to your family, stay cheerful and
write back

your old friend,
who is known in the village as
Don Jaime

Don Jaime

LETTER

3

AGAIN THE AUTHOR TO PAULINE

Contains the first story about a shepherd,
a goat and a mysterious island

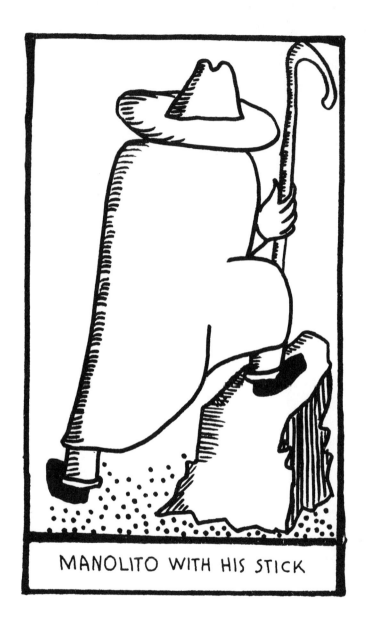

MANOLITO WITH HIS STICK

Dear Pauline,

Shortly after I mailed your letter, I spoke
with my neighbor, the shepherd Manolito,
about well-being and happiness. He told me a
story that I liked very much, mostly because
it fits right in with my thoughts about happiness. So, I want to write it down for you.
I add a picture of Manolito. Because it's hard
to draw his face, I have given you a picture
of his back. The story is called:

The Story of Manolito, the Shepherd

It is a funny thing about happiness, Señor. He who has it
doesn't notice it. He who is looking for it, doesn't find it.
Only he who has lost it, knows afterward that he once held
happiness for a moment in his hands.

With happiness, Señor, our fate seems to be like that of
the eighth Canary Island, which, as you know, carries the
beautiful name San Borodón. They say some piece of the
lost paradise can still be found there. Pirates who tried to
land on it in the sixteenth century found that a powerful

current made any landing impossible. Other great navigators—the Portuguese, if I'm right—also tried to land on the island. They had heard that everything there would be wonderful. But they, too, failed.

There are, Señor, many ballads, songs, and books about the Island San Borodón, but very few people can claim to have really seen it.

I am one of the few, one of those who has really seen it; it happened on a hot summer afternoon.

I had lost one of my goats, and I assumed it had climbed up the mountain. So I left the herd below to the care of my herd dogs and climbed a camel path to the top.

On the top of the ridge one can look across the sea toward the north. When I came to the top, I found my goat. But it behaved oddly. It didn't bleat when I came. It didn't graze. And it didn't try to run. It simply stood, motionless, like a statue, and looked out across the sea. I still remember that a light breeze was coming from the water and that cicadas hummed all around.

My eyes followed the goat's, looking over sea, and then, like the goat, I didn't feel the wind anymore or hear the sounds of the cicadas. It felt, Señor, as if land and sea were

holding their breath; for below me—almost reachable—
was an island in the blue water that I'd never seen before.
It formed a longish oval with four rivers crossing it, whose
waters sparkled in the sun. I saw seven towns on seven
hills. The shore nearest me was clothed in deepest green.
I've never seen such green on our island. There are, perhaps,
such green meadows in Europe, pastures of which my sheep
may only dream, because they'll never see them on these
islands. I saw, too, a path with a coach, a rider on a camel,
and a herd of snow-white sheep.

I cannot tell you, Señor, how long my goat and I stared
at the island. Maybe it was hours, maybe only seconds. I
only know that I said to my goat: "That down there, Pacharita, my little bird . . ." (That is the name of the goat.) ". . .
that down there, Pacharita, is San Borodón."

I said it quite simply, Señor, not being silly like the lady
tourists when they see our sunrise, nor reverent as some
priests when they give the blessing. I said it casually, as if
I had said that it was a nice day. At that moment, I was not
even aware of the great happiness that had come over me.

Only after I had said it did I realize that I had spoken
the name of the island. And at that moment the sea began

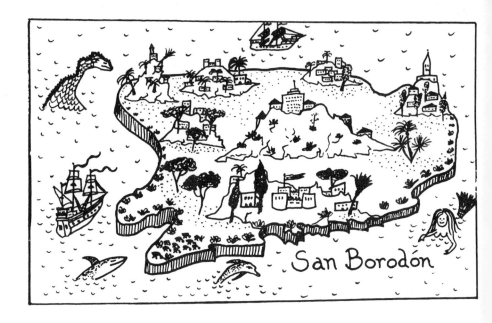

San Borodón

to foam and the island became wrapped in veils of spray.

All at once I heard the cicadas again, felt the wind from the water, and saw my goat move. It shook its head as if some pesky flies were bothering it, then jumped back down to the herd.

Amazed, I looked after it. Then I looked out at the sea. It was totally calm and blue and innocent under the sun. There were no waves, no foam, and I saw nothing on the water but a small white ship in the distance. The island, which I thought I had seen, was no longer there. Probably,

I decided, it was no more than my imagination; the sound of the cicadas and the shimmering heat had made me dream.

But when Pacharita, my goat, gave birth several days later to a sturdy, snow-white kid, an animal of a kind I had never had in a herd of mine, I was convinced that I had really and truly seen San Borodón.

Because with San Borodón, Señor, it is just as it is with happiness: One doesn't find it when one searches for it; one doesn't know it when one sees it; but afterwards, after the picture fades away, one knows one had seen it for a short, fleeting moment.

I wanted to add this story of Manolito's to my comments about well-being and happiness, Pauline, because stories are always better than theories.

Don't forget to write
to your old friend J.

Don Jaime

29

PAULINE TO THE AUTHOR

About giant families,
Holy Books,
the saintly Francis
and a business proposition

Dear Don Jaime,

How do you actually pronounce Jaime, and what does the word _Don_ mean? Many thanks for both letters! My giant family sends you their regards, too; but my father says that you, as a writer, should know that a large family is a gigantic family and not a giant family. Only giants can make a giant family!

Everything you wrote was very interesting. Saint Dolores is not in my calendar. (Her name is not in my Book of Saints either.) But just to let you know — I think the Book of Saints is very boring and I bought it only for Religious Instruction in school. I don't like so many holy items heaped in one place. I only like St. Francis, because he was good to animals. Here is a picture of him I drew for you.

Dear Don Jaime, I did buy the address labels; they are in this envelope. You don't

have to give back the money, says
my father. But you can write
me a story instead, because Manolito's
story was the best part of your
letters, and because I used to tell
you stories once for sweets. You
don't have to write long letters
about strange plants and Saint
Dolores. Only stories. One about
Saint Francis and the animals.
I'll be happy to buy other things for you
if you can't find them on your Canary Island
in return for stories. Then I'll have fun
and you'll have the things you need. And
then we'll both be happy. Please think
it over!
There is not much to tell about us.
Peter was in France, but he has not learned
much French, only some dirty words like

Farmer Hartl uses. Beate is in school, and Klaus is still as beastly to me as he was before.

Well, dear Don Jaime, stay well among your Jacarandas and other plants. Many regards.

from Your Pauline

LETTER

5

THE AUTHOR TO PAULINE

Gives an answer to the question
why one is called "Don,"
remarks about driving,
a story about the Saintly Francis
and a request for erasers

Me, stretched out on the beach near the water

Dear Pauline,

Very, very many thanks for the address labels, which I really needed very badly! Now all my packages and large envelopes can go out into the world beautifully labeled.

I have thought over your suggestion, and I agree: You send me sorely needed small items, and I'll send you stories in return.

A few days after I received your letter, I went down to a bathing beach and stretched out in the black sand with pad and pencil and began a story about the saintly Francis. But it got too hot to write. (Even though I was lying near the water, as my drawing shows.) So I jumped into the sea, and afterwards I went home and finished the story there. I did it in an easy chair on Terrace Number 11. I took great care with the story, as befits the saintly Francis. And when it was done, I put it aside for two days, and finally took it up to the bamboo pavillion on my roof, corrected it and changed it slightly.

Before I copy the story, I want to explain to you that the J in Spanish is pronounced like an H in English. So Jaime becomes Haime.

I can also tell you why they call me "Don." In Spain (Our island belongs geographically to Africa, but politically to Spain.), "Don" meant "Master" in the olden days. I live in a house high above the whole village, and I thought at first that that was why the people gave me the title "Don." But I was wrong. The reason is that I have a chauffeur for my car. There is a Spanish saying that says: "Un señor no porta." That means that a gentleman does not carry, nor haul, nor labor. Now if someone does not even touch the steering wheel of his car, but keeps a chauffeur for this purpose, then the people in the village think he has to be a very fine gentleman, and then, of course, one has to address him as "Don."

That I have a chauffeur because I am such a poor driver, does not make sense to the villagers. They are convinced that driving requires only a great intellect, and that I could drive if I really wanted to. I do not try to change their minds. Besides, I have

38

come to enjoy the luxury of being driven. I see
so much more than the man behind the wheel,
whose name is, by the way, Amado, and who knows
all the thousand curves on this island.
You see him in this picture.

And now after this explanation, here is
your story, which I have illustrated a bit.
It is called:

How St. Francis Preached to the Larks

One time, on a mild summer day, as St. Francis walked
across a field, he came upon a lark with a broken wing. He
was very sorry for the lark, for a lark that cannot rise
and sing is in a bad way, worse off than a worm or a bug
whose homes and happiness are in the ground. The good
Francis went over and touched the bird, and it became well
again.

"I want to thank you," twittered the lark. "But what is a
lark's gratitude? I'd rather do something for you!"

"He who does something good should not expect gratitude," replied St. Francis. "But maybe you can do me a

FRANCIS

BEFORE GIVING HIS SERMON

favor, not because you feel you must, but simply out of kindness!"

"Tell me your wish, kind man."

"Call your brothers and sisters, little bird, and permit me to deliver a sermon to them."

The little bird sighed. "Is that necessary?"

"No," answered St. Francis. "You need not listen. But I would like to tell you about the larks' heaven."

"That is a different story!" twittered the bird. "Wait here, and prepare your sermon."

Not an hour had passed before the field was carpeted with larks. They twittered and trilled and hopped and nodded around the holy man, as if the field itself were the larks' heaven.

Francis folded his hands to pray: "Our Father, in whom I believe, help me to find the right words. Amen."

The larks in the field lifted their heads during the prayer and kept very still. Then St. Francis began his sermon:

"Dear Sisters and Brothers of the air, look at the buzzard who circles above our heads. He wants to swoop down and eat one of you, but he does not dare. There are too many of you; he is afraid. Now you may think that this is how it will be in the larks' heaven: many larks, many singing voices, much happiness, and only buzzards who fear your numbers. But I tell you, there will be cats in the larks' heaven, too. Only they will not pursue you. In the larks' heaven there will be insects. But you will not eat them. Whosoever is hungry, will merely open his beak and the air will nourish him."

Some of the Larks sighed at the thought of so much happiness. But one male lark had some doubts. "What must we do to go to this heaven?" he twittered. "Pray and fast and eat no insects on Fridays?"

The holy man smiled at the bird's question and answered, "Do what you have been told: Be merry and sing. Then you can sing in the birds' paradise."

With that hundreds of birds flew into the summer sky and sang so beautifully that their song carried up into paradise.

St. Francis, still in the field, listened to them and said to himself, "Thank goodness I gave them only two command-ments: to be merry and to sing. That is what makes larks and people happy. And a longer sermon they would never have understood anyhow, for they do have small heads."

FRANCIS

AFTER GIVING HIS SERMON

 FRANCIS'S DREAM

That evening, as he lay in his cell at the monastery, the saint dreamed he was standing in the middle of the larks' paradise among hundreds of little birds who had sung their way into heaven.

I hope, Pauline, that you like this story, since it has only one very short sermon. (The Very Reverend Mooshammer should look upon this as an example.)

If you want to do me a favor, and if you want a new story besides, please consider that we have very poor erasers hereabouts and that I could do with some of the soft white ones you can buy so easily.

> Regards to your gigantic family
> and to yourself from your
> Don Jaime

Dou Jaime

PAULINE TO THE AUTHOR

About serious and playful stories,
skinned knees
and Pauline's thoughts about sports.

Dear Don Jaime,

Many thanks for your story about St. Francis. My father, whose name is Francis too, says that it really is a Franciscan story. I liked it even though normally I don't like holy stories. The next time, though, I'd rather have a story that is a little silly. You really do write those much better. For instance, that program you wrote with rabbits that sing. Write me the life of a rabbit singer. Of course, that's only a suggestion. If you don't want to, then write a different story, please.

Dear Don Jaime, I'll send you the erasers tomorrow. They will be an advance for the next story. The life of a rabbit singer would really interest me very much, but actually, any story you send me will make me very happy.

Do you always correct your stories?
And where is the eleventh terrace?

There isn't much news to tell you
from here. Beate does her homework
very nicely, and Klaus skinned his knee
playing soccer. You can see him here in
the picture. My mother says one can
overdo sports. But Harry, who is a real
athlete, says a true athlete sometimes has
to bleed. I am not much interested in
sports. I'd rather read stories
or sing.

Dear Don Jaime, it would be
very nice if you would write a story
for me about a singing rabbit.

Many regards from all of us.

Your Pauline

Klaus

LETTER

7

THE AUTHOR TO PAULINE

Remarks about athletes and goalies,
talent and hard work,
rivers and gorges,
garbage disposal every fifteen years
and the story about a singing rabbit.

Dear Pauline,

Our business deals really work extremely well. Your erasers are here, and my latest story is finished.

I have the same opinion about sports as you have. It doesn't seem too important to me if one man runs faster than another. Mostly I think it's the referees who make such a big fuss about everything. The athletes themselves often seem much more relaxed about it, and seem to be having fun. I have a great weakness for only one particular sport, water polo, a kind of basketball in the water. Whenever I can go to a game, I do—of course, only as a spectator. It is the goalies I like to watch. Even without firm ground under their feet, they leap high into the air to catch the ball and prevent a goal. To show you what I mean, I'll draw you a picture of a water polo goalie.

I expected Beate to do well in school, because she has to work hard for what she gets, and such people often succeed better than others. You did not have to work so hard and so

A WATER POLO GOALIE

sometimes you were negligent with your homework assignments.

But people like you, who have ability,
should not be proud of it. They did not make
it themselves. A person has talent, or he
doesn't. I do not feel proud because I have some
talent as storyteller. Only when I have re-
written a story, sometimes three, four, or even
ten times am I proud, because then I have
polished my talent enough to make it really
shine.

The new story, which you shall have for

your erasers, was actually written at <u>one</u>
sitting, on the 11th terrace whose location
you wanted me to describe.

Let me tell you a bit about the terrace
before I tell you the story of the rabbit
singer.

Our island was once lush and green and
crisscrossed with rivers that had cut themselves deep into the rocks. Today, these
rivers are dry. But the deep gorges where they
once flowed still crisscross the island.
The natives call them barrancos.

One of these gorges runs from the top of the
mountains behind me into the capital, Las
Palmas. On the bridge that spans the gorge near
the cathedral the tourist buses stop. The
guides announce through the microphone,
"Ladies and gentlemen, here you see what was
once a river; today it is the gorge of Guiniguada!" (The guides pronounce it Gi-ni-gu-
a-da.)

This gorge, Pauline, runs eastward right
next to my house. If I lean over the wall of
terrace number 12 I can see down some forty or

THE GORGE AT GUINIGUADA

fifty feet. And there below are pebbles, rocks, bushes, little trees and the garbage of my household, which my maids dump down there—naturally, since we have no garbage disposal. (Every fifteen years, when there is a hard rain that makes the gorge into a river again, the garbage is washed away.) On the other side of the gorge a steep rock wall rises, which I have tried to draw for you, in part.

To make a long story short: Just above the gorge lies terrace number 12 of my house, and within that terrace, somewhat elevated, lies terrace number 11, which has morning sun. I like to sit there after breakfast in a deck chair, under the lemon trees, with a writing pad on my knees. This is where I composed and illustrated the latest story for you. Here it is:

The Rabbit with Hiccups

A boy-rabbit wanted to become a singer. His aim was to become a tenor at most famous of all the rabbit operas, the

Long-Ear Scala. This was, as all connoisseurs of long-ear music know, no small ambition, but in this case it seemed perfectly feasible. It was generally agreed that the young rabbit possessed excellent "vocal powers," as all his teachers said, and a special "timbre." His breath-control was admirable. As soloist in the Hobblestone Boys' Choir, he received the highest praise from the bunny Field and Stream press.

But as this promising rabbit got older, he found himself in the dangerous period when his voice was changing. It either broke or squeaked high and loud over the voices of other rabbits. And again and again a nasty hiccup would find its way into his speech and unfortunately into his songs, too.

The young rabbit finally went to his voice teacher and said, always interrupted by hiccups, "Mr. Humpelman, it makes no, hicc, forgive me, sense for me to study under you right now. When a voice is changing, it's imposs-hicc-ible to sing."

"Yes, yes, my boy," said teacher Humpelman. "Let's stop the lessons for a while until your voice has outgrown this change."

Almost a half a year passed before the change was over. But unfortunately the young rabbit's ridiculous and annoying hiccup seemed to have settled in for good. Whatever his voice had gained in ripeness and roundness was destroyed by his eternal hiccups. When he sang the famous aria from the first act of the opera "Lampedon and Lampedusa," it went:

O Lampedu-hicc-se,
You are my mu-hicc-se,
You're my muse-hicc and my light.
O be mi-hicc-ne,
And I'll be thi-hicc-ne!
Without your smile I cannot-hicc fight

Humpelman, the voice teacher, was terribly upset when he heard this. The young rabbit was also upset. And everyone of any name or rank in the rabbits' music world wrung his paws to think that such an outstanding talent was being destroyed by those ridiculous hiccups. Famous ear-nose-and-throat specialists tried to cure the young singer with all kinds of medicine. Rabbit psychiatrists and psychologists

58

PROFESSOR
HUMPELMAN

HICCKY,
THE DETECTIVE

were consulted; specialists for voice formation tried their hand; but everything failed. When the young singer after months of silence finally opened his mouth again, he spoke the sentence that later became famous: "Hicc believe hicc am healed."

In short, the hiccups were still there.

What to do? Finally the voice coach had a splendid idea. He wrote a long article about his protégé for the opera magazine for rabbits, "Polybunnia," describing the young rabbit's promising career. The article ended with an unintelligible sentence: "If one can't sail against the wind one must sail with it! Hicc!"

No rabbit who read the article really understood it. It was not until several months later that the musical rabbits saw what the teacher had meant. At that time they viewed the opening of the now well-known comic crime-opera "Hic, the Rabbit Detective." It was offered with a superb, glittering cast. The lead was sung by no one but the promising young rabbit, of course, with hiccup.

The result was unbelievable. There were more than one hundred curtain calls. The audience applauded till their paws ached. Huccupping became fashionable among rabbits, and a record company made several million rabbit dollars with the Hicc aria:

> Seven and seventy tricky cases
> Our great Hiccky solved himself.
> Seven and seventy hard-boiled criminals
> He laid upon the jailer's shelf.
> Seven and seventy nut-hard cases
> Our great Hiccky, full of stealth.
> Seven and seventy stumbling blocks
> Hiccky kicked off by himself,
> Hiccky kicked off,
> Hiccky kicked off,
> Tricky Hiccky
> by himself!

The young rabbit became the leading singer in the field of Comic Opera, one of the best loved rabbit singers of his time.

Need it be said that Hiccky was a triumphant success at Long-Ear Scala, too, and that special Hiccky-Operas were written just for him.

His old teacher wrote a voluminous biography of his pupil, in which he said, "What endears our singer to the hearts of young and old, simple and refined, is not only his vocal ability but also the refreshing hiccup of his childhood days, which he kept into maturity."

As you can see, Pauline, I've tried, in return for your erasers, to give you the life story of a singing rabbit as well as I could. Whether or not you find the story silly enough is for you to decide. I have at least tried.

Stay well, Pauline, and see if you can get some black carbon paper for me, and give my regards to your gigantic family.

Warm regards from your
Don Jaime

Dou Jaime

PAULINE TO THE AUTHOR

About black carbon paper,
family poets,
Miss Hirsch
and rhymed compositions

Dear Don Jaime,

My father read the story of the Singing Rabbit to all of us, putting in some marvellous hiccs. Beate choked on a piece of apple, and Klaus had to hit her hard on the back so she could breathe again. You can see her here in the picture. We bought your black carbon paper right away, which I'll enclose here. For this we would like to have a story about a mouse and an elephant, if you feel like it. Perhaps you could think of one. My father says you are a poet for the whole family, because Harry listened, too, and he is already eighteen.

I would like to play in your gorge, Guiniguada, which is pronounced Gi-ni-gu-a-da. Or does one get bitten there by rats? Are there caves in the wall that one can climb into?

I am going to remember your sentence that says one must try to sail with the wind when one can't sail against it. We had to write a composition for Miss Hirsch. So I wrote a poem, and she gave me a D— and wrote under it that I was too young to write rhymes and a composition was too serious a thing to be done in rhyme. So I wrote the next composition for her without rhymes and got a B+. I'm sailing with the wind and will now draw you a picture of Miss Hirsch.

Dear Don Jaime, since we're sending the black carbon paper, it would be nice, if we could have a story about a mouse and an elephant. We are all waiting eagerly for it, and send you our regards, but especially

Your Pauline

Miss Hirsch

p.s. The Most Reverend Mooshammer says that animals don't go to heaven. Is that true?

LETTER

9

THE AUTHOR TO PAULINE

Contains wise thoughts about laughter,
playing in gorges,
about caves and German teachers
and the story of the mouse and the elephant

Dear Pauline,

It is nice that Beate choked on an apple! Excuse me! I meant to say that it's nice that she laughed so hard at my story that a piece of apple got stuck in her throat. Laughing brings fresh air, high spirits, and, of course, charm. (Except when it is done out of malice.)

The carbon paper has arrived. I don't say "thank you" because my thanks are in the story about the mouse and the elephant, which I wrote on terrace number 2 sitting on my glider. I'll copy it for you, but first I want to answer some of your questions.

You can certainly play in my gorge without having to be afraid of rats. The only danger is the neighbors, who are used to throwing broken brooms, empty boxes, empty bottles, old baby carriages, vegetable peelings and rusted iron poles down into the gorge. All of this might hit you. People here do whistle before they throw; but you have to whistle back immediately to keep them from throwing. I don't know if you can whistle, and I have no idea if your reflexes are quick enough to save

ENTRANCE TO A CAVE IN ATENARA

you. So I don't recommend playing in the
gorge, which is, after all, a good thousand
miles away from you, any way.

There are some caves in the walls of the
gorge to the north of my house. But they smell,
so no one ever goes inside. However there
are caves above the gorge in the rocky cliffs
near the village of Angostura that are quite
easy to enter. They are cemented inside and
used for housing people.

You would never believe that these houses
were actually caves if you just looked at the
pretty facades. You can only tell they are

69

CAVE DWELLING IN ANGOSTURA

caves when you go inside. And even so they have
normal whitewashed walls. But only a few
very poor people live in caves, for they are
after all nothing but rock-holes and quite
damp. I have drawn one of them for you. Here
it is.

The note Miss Hirsch put on your rhymed
composition is a little upsetting. She must
mean that a composition is a very serious
undertaking, and a poem is nothing but a pretty
game. Once in a while it may be so. But it is
more often the other way around. I will try to
answer your question about animals in heaven

with a rhymed composition. But first I have to think seriously about it. I'll send you the story as soon as it's finished so you can show it to Miss Hirsch. But don't expect it right away. It may take me a while.

Now let me copy down and illustrate the "Family Story" for you. Here it is:

The Mouse and the Elephant

A very young elephant had lost its way and was wandering through town looking for something to eat. He was hungry. As he plodded along an elderly mouse ran right in front of him and was almost squashed to death.

"Why don't you look where you're stepping, you giant baby?" screeched the mouse. "Where are your eyes?"

"In my head," replied the elephant politely. "But they are dimmed by hunger pains."

"So, you are hungry," murmured the mouse, who immediately felt like a mother to the baby elephant. "If that is true, child, it seems that I, as an older person, ought to do something for you. But what?"

Thoughtfully the mouse looked at the elephant's long trunk. Then her whiskers perked up as if they were a radar antennae receiving an idea.

"An elephant as a household appliance," she said quietly, almost to herself. "That wouldn't be too bad."

"Come, child!" she shouted up to the elephant. "I think I have something for you. I hope you can keep up with me."

"I shall try my best, madam," said the elephant, and he followed with a deliberate step by step, after the quickly scurrying mouse.

They went together to a tall apartment house. There the mouse said, "If you would be so kind, child, as to take me up on your trunk, we could go up to the sixth floor together."

So the elephant took the mouse on the tip of his trunk, and trying not to let the trunk sway too much, carried the mouse to the sixth floor, where the elephant, at the mouse's request, pressed a door bell.

A friendly, white-haired lady answered the door and said, "Good . . . oh!"

"This is a hungry young elephant," explained the mouse

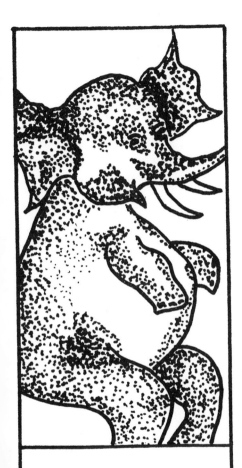

THE ELEPHANT

THE MOUSE

on the trunk. "How do you do, Mrs. Pfaefflinger?"

The lady, who saw the mouse only after she spoke, replied: "How have you been. Mrs. Fallmayer?"

"One squeaks along," peeped the mouse. "I want to introduce my friend, the dust-sucker. He is hungry and needs a job."

"How much does it take to feed you, young man?" asked the lady.

"I don't need much, Madam. Two bales of hay a day."

"What a coincidence!" cried the lady. "My brother has a farm outside of town. He has rented out eight fields to some sport clubs. But he doesn't know what to do with the grass he has to cut. He needs a ball boy, too, for the tennis players. How does that sound?"

"Exactly the right thing for my friend," screeched the mouse delightedly. "What is the address?"

The lady explained how to get to the farm, and still sitting on the trunk, the mouse directed the elephant there. The elephant followed the directions, and very soon they found the fields they were looking for.

Both the lady and gentleman sports lovers were delighted with the elephant. He was not only good as a ball boy, but

74

he also saved them from having to roll the tennis courts by stamping on them. And in addition to all that, he took care of the problem of hay disposal, because he ate it. The mouse had brought him at the right time to the right place.

"Madam, how can I thank you?" said the elephant, deeply moved.

"By letting me off your trunk," said Frau Fallmayer, the mouse. "I became a bit airsick when you became happy and began to swing it."

"Oh pardon, madam!" said the young elephant, dismayed. "In my happiness I forgot . . ."

"It's all right, my child," interrupted the mouse. "The main thing is that you are happy and content."

And that the elephant certainly was and remained. He was a most cheerful and contented multipurpose elephant. And every Sunday he let the six-to-ten-year-old boys ride on his back and swing from his trunk.

"When one is young, one should trust older persons," he always said. "Then all problems are solved!"

With this wisdom from a young elephant I
close my letter, Pauline, wishing all of you
much fun in reading it aloud,

> and am with good wishes, as always,
> your Don Jaime

P.S.: I have a new story in mind; but it's hard
for me to write with unbrushed teeth. I have
just used the last of my toothpaste and I can't
find any here. Mr. Gensch at the drugstore
knows what kind I use. If you would send some
to me, I could write again.

Don Jaime

PAULINE TO THE AUTHOR

About silly stories,
free toothpaste,
caves and houses

My Cave

1) Living cave   2) Bed cave   3) Play cave
4) Cave for making noise   5) Doll's cave
6) Leomonade cave   7) Garage cave

Dear Don Jaime,

Mutti says the story of the mouse and the elephant is very good because we can learn from it that physical size is not too important in life but cleverness and experience are. Mutti wants us to learn somthing from every story. I don't. I like so much to have fun. Couldn't you write a fun-story? Maybe you could write one that didn't have a beginning or an ending so there wouldn't be anyplace for a lesson.

Since you can't write with unbrushed teeth, I'm sending some toothpaste that Mr. Densch gave me. It is free. For this you are to autograph a book for his daughter when you are here.

You don't have to be afraid to let me play in your gorge, because I can whistle very loud. If people whistle before throwing down their iron poles, I will whistle right back. That'll make them watch out.

I want to see the caves in Angostura when I come to see you. I have never seen a cave house. My father says a couple of thousand years ago people here lived in caves, too. Too bad we have houses now.

I have drawn a picture of the kind of cave I would like. Write me when such a cave is available. My father and Harry would build the doors and windows for it. Or are caves very expensive, just like houses? If so, I will have to wait until I'm bigger and can earn money.

Dear Don Jaime, I am really looking forward to your rhymed composition because I want to know why animals can't go to heaven. Would you please think of a silly story, too? You should have the toothpaste by now!

It's getting very cold here now, and the trees are almost all bare. Beate got a B in spelling, but Klaus got a D, the lazybones.

Well Don Jaime, keep brushing your teeth so you can write stories, and once more, a hug to you from all of us.

Many regards,
Your Pauline

THE AUTHOR TO PAULINE

Contains remarks about
everything that has an end,
the use of windows,
dictation marks and the story of a useful octopus

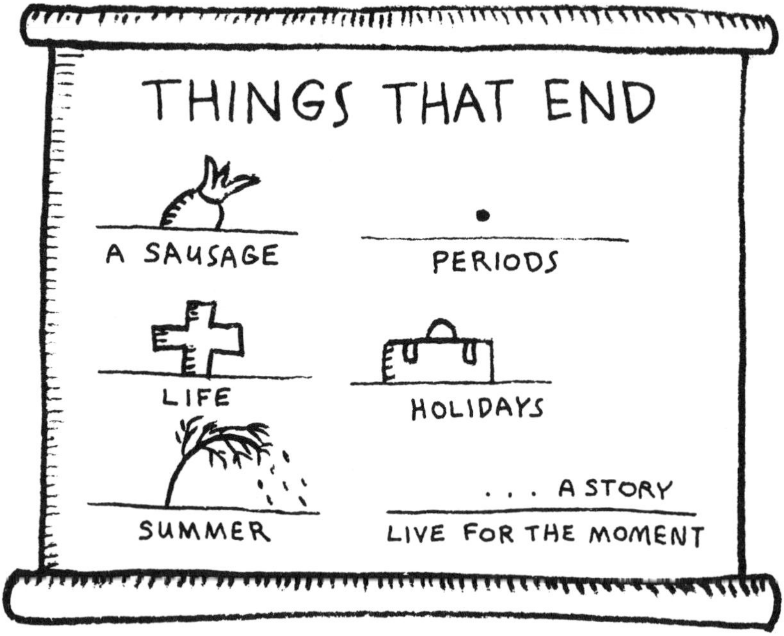
THINGS THAT END
A SAUSAGE
PERIODS
LIFE
HOLIDAYS
SUMMER
. . . A STORY
LIVE FOR THE MOMENT

Dear Pauline,

With brushed teeth (Please thank Mr. Gensch for the toothpaste.) I have been on terrace number 11 trying to write a Silly Story, one without beginning or end, but it was not easy. I don't like stories without a beginning. I do like introductions (the more intricate the better). So I gave my story an exceptionally intricate introduction, one that is not really a true beginning. (That is what you wanted.) It was difficult, though, not to give the story an end, for almost everything has an end: the sausage, the composition, life, the vacations, the summer and a story, too. (You can see that from my pictures.)

But because everything always keeps going ahead anyhow, sausage making, the writing of compositions, life, vacation plans, and storytelling, it is possible to write a story without an end. A story can go on and on like the story about the chicken that lays an egg from which a chicken comes, which lays an egg, from which a chicken comes, which again lays an egg from which a chicken . . .

You do understand, don't you?

That you'd like to live in a cave is understandable. As a child I used to build caves in our attic. But as a grown-up I like to see what is going on and so I like to look out of the window. Sometimes that is difficult in caves.

Your plan for a children's cave is very nicely thought out, and I will try to find a suitable cave for you. But unfortunately they are not inexpensive because rich people in Las Palmas are now trying to buy summer caves. That has made cave prices go up, unfortunately.

You wrote me the spelling marks of Beate and Klaus, but not your own. Was it that bad?

Here is my silly story. I have copied it carefully for you. Do read with care:

Polly Plauz, the Useful Octopus

Polly Plauz was an unusually large octopus, when she lay down on her stomach, or to be exact when she stood on her head, or rather when she propped herself on her chin, no, when she spread her eight arms and lay on the floor, or rather stood, no, squatted, or let's say found herself on the floor. When she found herself—like an eight-pointed star —on the floor, she was from the end of one arm to the end of the arm directly opposite all of thirty feet long.

So our story can rightly begin with the assumption that Polly Plauz was indeed an unusually large octopus.

But in spite of this, Polly Plauz had a pleasing disposition. I mean—and again to be exact—she was quiet and lovable, not because of but rather in spite of her size; for large animals (and even men) such as elephants and weight-lifters are often pleasant. So Polly Plauz was kind and did not feel overly important because of her size. In fact, no one was more modest or kinder than she.

That is really all one ought to know about this octopus to understand why she suddenly became a useful octopus on the pier in Casablanca. Except for one characteristic of

Polly Plauz that I forgot to mention: her almost addictive interest in people. She was—again to be more specific—terribly curious about anything pertaining to people. She had—even though she was a water animal—the deepest interest in everything people were doing. With that in mind, it ought to be clear what I mean when I say that Polly Plauz was people-struck.

Polly Plauz was on the pier whenever a large ship arrived or departed (somewhat like families here who go to the station to watch people arrive and depart) along with the customs inspector, the harbormaster, and the loading inspector.

There is, however, a dancing couple, with whom the story really begins. They did not seem to see Polly Plauz when they stood for the first time on the pier at Casablanca with their six suitcases. It is important for the story to know that their names were Angela and Enrique and that they performed their act together as a pair. Angela was always absentminded and highly nervous. Enrique, her partner, was attentive and kept saying, "Yes, dear," to all her demands.

With one of Miss Angela's demands our story now be-

POLLY ON THE PIER

gins. She asked somewhat reproachfully: "Enrique, are all the pieces here? Have you asked for a porter?"

To this, Enrique answered as usual: "Yes, dear!"

That's how it happened that Miss Angela—who we know was highly nervous and absentminded—assumed that the arm that came from the right was the arm of the porter. She pointed to a large steamer trunk and said, "Take this one first. Our cabin aboard ship is number seven. And then take this basket here."

When a second arm reached for the basket, the lady dancer paid little attention and added, "This wooden case is ours, too, and also the tin box and the small case with the plaid cloth cover."

She still paid no attention when a third and fourth arm started to reach for things. Only when a fifth arm seized her hatbox did she become suspicious, because a porter usually has only two arms and two hands. She turned her head to the right with raised eyebrows and . . .

As I said, she didn't know Polly Plauz and was, as has been stated here several times, very nervous and highly excitable. Is it any wonder then, that she fainted at the sight of Polly Plauz? The only amazing thing is that she had time to call out, "Enrique, catch me!"

The dancer said as usual, "Yes, dear!" But, also as usual, he didn't bother to look.

So Polly Plauz used her sixth arm, the only one that was still free, to catch the falling dancer. (Arms seven and eight she needed to keep herself on her feet, or rather on her arms, or rather, shall we say, to keep upright.)

Of course, all this was slightly new for the octopus Polly Plauz. Never before had she stood on the pier with five pieces of luggage and an unconscious dancer in six of her arms. So she asked in her own modest way: "Excuse me, Mr. Enrique, could you give me a hand with one piece of luggage, your wife, perhaps? I only have six arms at my disposal."

The dancer was just about to say, "Yes dear," when he remembered that his wife had only two arms and it could not have been his wife who had just spoken.

So he turned his head to the left instead of the right as before.

When he saw the octopus, who in addition to five pieces of luggage was holding his wife, he immediately offered to carry something, too, and picked up the little case with

POLLY AT WORK

the plaid cloth cover, the only thing left. Then he went aboard, and Polly Plauz meekly followed him, swaying slightly under the weight of Angela and the rest of the luggage.

That's how it came about that the octopus, Polly Plauz, became a truly useful octopus. And that should be the end of the story.

That Polly Plauz stayed with the dancing couple and their six pieces of luggage and traveled with them throughout Europe can be reported only because not one of the three was able to change his or her ways. Angela continued to be absentminded and Enrique helpful and inattentive, and Polly, who was both helpful and curious about people, could not bear to see the two people and their luggage standing around harbors, railroad stations or airports with no one to help them.

As time went by the attitudes of the three toward each other improved somewhat; but, basically, they remained just about as they had been in the beginning. Miss Angela always started when she saw the gigantic octopus offering her six arms helpfully. Again and again Angela called, "Enrique, haven't you finally been able to find a porter to

free us of this huge slimy animal?" (She had read in the dictionary that octopi are slimy.)

And Enrique always answered, "Yes (or as the case might be) no, dear!" But he never did anything, and there was little for Polly Plauz to do but sigh as she took care of the luggage. As time went on she became quite adept at her work. She finally considered herself as a seventh piece of luggage and protected herself by hanging a sign around her neck, or the lower part of her head, that said:

CAREFUL! ARTISTS' LUGGAGE! LIVING ANIMAL!

It should not be left unsaid—even though the story was ended long ago—that Enrique and Angela soon became well known as the dancers with the octopus trunk. As such, they received more money than ever before, but they had to spend a lot of money feeding Polly Plauz, who was a picky eater and did not hesitate to say she couldn't stand anything that smelled of herring.

It should be mentioned, too, that Angela, three times a week, pressed some money into one of the arms of the octopus so she could take a bath in an indoor pool, a public pool, or if necessary in a bathtub (because Angela had read that octopi are normally water animals).

In spite of all this one can't assume that the three lived happily with one another. They just accepted their lot—like many people—but they sighed about it fairly often.

Actually Polly Plauz would have much preferred living in the Atlantic and occasionally pulling herself up on the dock at Casablanca to carrying artists' luggage. But since Polly, as earlier stated, was very accomodating, and since Enrique, in spite of the repeated pleadings of his highly nervous and absentminded wife, seemed incapable of calling for a porter, Polly Plauz is a well-trained luggage octopus, still carrying . . . and so . . .

And so it is a story without end—like so many stories on this funny earth.

You see, Pauline, the story has—as you wanted—no end. But now the time has come to end at least this letter.

I'm sending all of you my warmest greetings. For my next story I would like a pencil sharpener with a plastic bowl attached to it (for the shavings), and I wish you in spite of cold weather and bare trees from the sunny isles

everything good, as your
Don Jaime

Don Jaime

12

PAULINE TO THE AUTHOR

*About pencil sharpeners with plastic containers,
stories from which one cannot learn anything
and about nonesense and nonsense*

Dear Don Jaime,

I'll send you a pencil sharpener with a plastic container (for the shavings) separately. Because it won't fit into an envelope.

Imagine! My father said after reading the story of the multi-purpose octopus, "Yes, that's the way life is. People don't change. Everyone stays just as he is, and so we keep moving in a perpetual carousel." (I had to look up the spelling of the word carousel in a dictionary.) What do you think about that! We even had to learn something from your nonsense story.

Can't you write a story from which one definitely cannot learn anything?

Maybe you could write one about an animal that does not exist? Or is that asking for too much for a pencil sharpener with a plastic container? Anyhow, Don Jaime, now you know what I would like.

I have thought it over and have decided that I wouldn't like to live in a cave, because I like to look out of windows, too, particularly in the back, and that's impossible in caves.

There is snow in the air here, says my grandfather. It would be nice to be on your island where I could swim. Do you have a nice beach? I have been to the ocean only once, and that was when I was very small. I liked it then very much.

Harry said yesterday that the story about the octopus is nonsense. I told him that you'd written it as a nonsense story just for me. Harry said, "Nonsense and nonsense are two different things."

I have drawn a picture of the way he looked

when he said it.

My brother   Harry

It made me happy to know that he
didn't learn anything from the story. For
him it was really a nonsense story.

Dear Don Jaime, please think about
an animal that isn't. You might be able
to write about one on your Terrace Number
11, because you get so many ideas there.

I didn't tell you about my spelling
grade because we had no spelling. On the
last test, I made a C.

When you lie at the beach please
think of cold Germany, and

Your Pauline

THE AUTHOR TO PAULINE

Clever sentences about nonsense
and the game and the story of the Birzel

Dear Pauline,

Thank you for your letter! The pencil sharpener hasn't arrived yet, but the Birzel has been found. I'll write to you about it at the end of my letter.

The fact that your father found something to be learned from the octopus story is not too surprising. Nonsense stories are, if you look at them closely, rather serious. They belong in the category play, sub-division nonsense. But people and animals all learn a lot from play: to speak, to eat, to fly, to walk, and to use their hands.

If your brother Harry calls the octopus story nonesense, he probably means something else. I suppose he thinks the story is silly, maybe because he has no talent for play. After all, he is dead serious about sports. He forgets the Olympics are called Olympic games, not Olympic duties. You might explain that to him.

I assume the snow your grandfather smelled in the air has fallen by now. There are, in any case, many German tourists here already, fleeing from the winter.

By the way, we have not one beach here, as you seem to think, but over thirty, some with black sand, some with white sand. The largest, most famous one is many miles long. It has very white sand, a beautiful boardwalk with many lights, and a long reef that not only breaks the waves but also keeps away sharks and the stinging jellyfish who burn your skin with their stringy underside. I would draw this beach for you, but then I would have to include the city of Las Palmas behind, with its tall hotels and narrow cavernous streets. And I don't have enough room for all that.

So instead I'll draw some pictures and introduce the following story to you as:

The Birzel

All foresters say the birzel is an unusual animal, especially on Thursdays, especially between the hours of 9:05 and 9:25 in the morning. So I was glad to see a birzel on a

Friday at 12:00, because Friday is close to Thursday, and 12:00 is close to 9:25.

The birzel was happy, too, to see me. It said, "One does not usually meet you on Friday."

"Yes," I answered, "I write stories most of the time."

"I thought so," said the birzel. "On the middle finger of your right hand, close to the nail, you have a hi. That comes from writing."

"I have a what on the right middle finger, Birzel?"

"A hi. That is a very, very small hill. That is why I left the *ll* out. Did you know the hi is a callous?"

"Yes," I said as I looked at my right middle finger. "The hi is really a callous. You have good eyes, Birzel."

"All of us foxes have good eyes."

"Are you really a fox?" I asked.

"Well," said the birzel, slightly embarrassed, "of course I'm not a real fox, rather a sea-el, wouldn't you think?"

"I don't know what a sea-el is," I said.

"A sea-el," explained the birzel, "is the front half of a Sea-Elephant. Don't you think there is a definite resemblance?"

"No!" I said. "Not at all. For one thing, you are much

too small."

"Am I really?" asked the birzel. "Then what am I like? I would really like to know which animal I resemble. Maybe a tiger? What do you think? Am I tiger-like?"

I looked closely at the birzel and answered, "There is a faint resemblance to a tiger, though of course, in mini-size."

"So you think so, too!" cried the birzel excitedly. "You also see a likeness to a tiger?"

"Who else noticed it?" I asked.

"My friend Ho," said the birzel.

"And who is that?"

"Ho is the front part of a horse," said the birzel. "I always talk to his front part, you know."

"It's hard to talk to his back part, Birzel."

"Huh! I didn't know that," said the birzel. "But I have to run to get to my hole in the ree."

"And that is probably the lower part of a tree," I remarked.

"Yes," said the birzel, very surprised. "How did you know?"

"One learns things when one befriends a birzel," I

BIRZEL'S HOLE IN THE REE

answered.

"I'm glad to hear it, my friend. I'm really very glad. Maybe we should take a train ride together. I can go to my hole some other time."

"But Birzel, we are in the forest. There is no train here."

"That's too bad!" said the birzel, looking very perturbed. "Every time I feel like doing something, that 'something' isn't there. Now there is not even a train here."

"But there are mushrooms, snails, ferns and . . ."

". . . and Birzel," completed the birzel.

"Yes," I said, "there is a birzel in this forest, too. And that is really the most amazing thing of all."

"Why is that so amazing?" asked the birzel.

"Because birzels are rare, Birzel. I only know one, namely you."

"Now that I think about it," said the birzel, "you are right. I, too, know only one birzel, namely me. And I'm not quite sure that I am really a birzel."

"Come, come," I said. "That you are a birzel is the only thing we know about for sure. Ask all the other animals in the forest. They'll tell you."

"All right," said the birzel. "Let's ask the others. Let's

BIRZEL IN THE FOREST

go first to the owl."

So we went to the owl, who was snoring in his tree. Even his snoring sounded like hooting, "Whoo-hoo, whoo-hoo."

"Whoo-hoo!" shouted the birzel.

Without answering the owl opened his left eye.

So I called, "Whoo-hoo," too.

Then the owl also opened his right eye, yawned, and asked, "What is so important that you must disturb my sleep?"

"Tell me who I am," called the birzel.

"You?" asked the owl, looking down from the tree with his big eyes. "You want to know who you are?"

"Yes," said the birzel impatiently. "Who am I?"

"That is no easy question," replied the owl. "Especially when one has just been sleeping soundly. I would say you are an animal."

"I know that myself," said the birzel, who was growing more and more impatient. "But what kind of animal?"

"That is not an easy question," said the owl. "I know that everybody calls you the birzel. But what is a birzel? And what does the word birzel mean? Let me sleep for a while. Maybe it will come to me in a dream."

BIRZEL'S FRIEND, HO

BIRZEL'S FRIEND OWL

RABBIT

BIRZEL TIME

The owl closed his eyes, and seconds later he had resumed his snoring.

The birzel said, "It's always the same with the owl. When you need him he sleeps, and when he's awake he confuses all the world with his speeches."

"But he did tell you, Birzel, that you are a birzel."

"What do you mean?" shouted the birzel." He said only that everyone knows me by that name. But he doesn't know what a birzel is! And he doesn't know what my name is either."

The poor animal was terribly upset. So I said, "Let's go to see Rabbit. Rabbit is an animal who confuses no one, and he can answer almost every question."

"All right," said the birzel. "Let's go and see Rabbit."

So we walked to the slope at the end of the woods where Rabbit always waits for the blue hare. We said, "How do you do Rabbit? Hasn't the blue hare come yet?"

"No," said the rabbit. "He is *really* very late. I am beginning to lose my patience."

"Before you lose it, I'd like to ask you a question," said the birzel.

"All right, do it quickly!"

113

"Well, Rabbit, I'd like to know who I am."

"You are the birzel," answered the rabbit without hesitation. "But if you want to know your name, too, I must tell you I don't know. And now I have to run, because I'm losing my patience. As you know, I'm waiting for the blue hare."

With these words the rabbit turned away, and the birzel and I went back into the forest.

"Now we know no more than before," I said.

"What do you mean?" asked the birzel. "Now I finally know what a birzel is, and what I am called."

"And, if you please, what is a birzel?"

"A birzel is a birzel," said the birzel happily.

"And what is your name?"

"I don't know."

"So you still don't know your name!"

"But I do!" said the birzel, who was beginning to grow impatient. My name is Idon'tknow. I am the birzel Idon't-know. Don't you see? And now I have to go to my cave to memorize my name. Anyhow, today is, Friday, the day I don't like to talk with people. Good-bye!"

In a moment the birzel was gone, and all I could hear

BIRZEL ON THE ROAD ∽

was his endless murmur: "Idon'tknow, Idon'tknow . . ."
Then I didn't hear anything more.

And I never saw the birzel again.

In case the birzel should come your way,
Pauline, give him my regards!

>   Best regards to you and yours, your
>   Don Jaime

P.S.: If you think about the fact that we often
have power shortages, you will understand
why a box of dripless candles would be very
handy.

>   T.A.
>   (the aforementioned)

Don Jaime

PAULINE TO THE AUTHOR

About dripless candles,
birzels,
the Most Reverend Mooshammer,
a snowman and a crow

Dear Don Jaime,

I hope you find this letter among the dripless candles! I'll tell you what I'd like in return for them at the end of this letter.

I saw the birzel yesterday. It is still memorizing its name and says nothing but, "I don't know." But it did not look like a small tiger to me, instead it looked like a smooth-shaven porcupine. I have drawn it here for you.

my friend

The Birzel

My family has been birzeling a lot. Even Harry said yesterday, "I'm going ska now." He only wanted to skate for a short time so he left off the rest of the word skating! I think he does have a sense of humor.

Beate's whole class birzels, too. When she goes to school, she says, "We are going to schoo", because she only uses the front entrance. And Beate's teacher said, "Now we will write some spe", because it was only a short list of spelling words.

The snow has arrived. We have built a snowman already. Yesterday and today both a crow sat on his head. I think it was the same crow. Maybe she is talking to the snowman.

Dear Don Jaime, I would like to know what a crow talks to a snowman about. Can you think about that on your sunny island? If so please write me a story about it. For the non-dripping candles.

How far have you gotten with your rhymed composition about the animals who don't get into Paradise? Can Saint Francis be in it, too? Or is that asking for too much?

I read your last letter to the Most Reverend Mooshammer. He told me to give you ki re, that means kind regards, because you are not a Catholic. He bizgels too, now.

Right now I do not want   want your bathing beach, because we are sleigh riding and skating. But I hope you have some happy waves and that you will send a new story about the snowman and a crow.

Many nice regards from all of us.

Your Pauline

THE AUTHOR TO PAULINE

Contains ki re to the Most Reverend Mooshammer,
notices about a flight to Africa and
a story from the Sahara desert

Dear Pauline,

Are you still birzeling? I have not met the birzel since the day I told you about, even though I was in a palm forest on Thursday at 9:15 sharp. But a grove of palm trees is probably not a forest. And I'm afraid the birzel knows it. (A picture of the palm grove is enclosed.) By the way, the birzel I met looked quite different from the one you drew. Is that because of the birzel or because of Pauline?

Please give the Most Reverend Mooshammer ki re from me, too. We used to be neighbors. His mailbox was next to mine.

I'm almost finished with the rhymed composition about animals and paradise. I don't really know when it will be done, though, because I'm flying to Africa next week. Maybe, you'll have my poem before I leave.

It is very easy to invent a snowman story here. On a sunny isle one can use one's imagination much better. And that is half the story.

But I don't have to imagine you a snowman story because my friend Brahim in the Sahara

PALM TREES WITHOUT BIRZEL

told me a story during his last visit about a
snowman and crows.

    I'll pass it on to you:

The Story of Brahim, the Moor

Brahim, the moorish trader, poured me a tiny glass of fresh aromatic tea. We were sitting in a room behind his shop, which was filled with precious oriental rugs. It stood in a settlement at the western border of the Sahara.

"Are the storytellers still coming through?" I asked him.

"No," said the Brahim. "They have gone back to the center of the desert, to the Tuaregs, to escape radios and newspapers. Since we have both here, they do not like us at all."

"That's too bad," I said.

"Why is too bad?" asked Brahim.

"Because I would have liked to hear one of their stories."

"Oh," said Brahim, "I know their stories well. I was born in the desert and I heard them as a child. Have another sip of tea, and I'll tell you a story."

With one practiced toss, Brahim sent the wide sleeves of his robe neatly over his shoulders to keep his arms and hands free to tell the story. Then he began.

The Story of the Lion and the Waterhole:

A lion once lived deep in the desert where one normally

BRAHIM

only sees jackals, hyenas, desert foxes and, once in a while, a gazelle. This lion was a loner who found food in a very simple way.

Since there was only one very small waterhole for miles around—it was not even big enough to be called a oasis— the lion had only to lie down right next to the waterhole as soon as it became dark and wait for a thirsty animal he could slay and eat.

One evening, though, three animals appeared at the waterhole at the same time, a desert fox, a jackal and a gazelle.

Since all three would have tasted equally good to the lion, he simply placed himself before them and said, "If I were so minded, all three of you could become my prey. But I will give you an opportunity to save yourselves. Each one of you is to tell me a lie. He who is the poorest liar will be eaten. You begin, desert fox."

The desert fox, who like the other two animals realized that he could not escape the lion should he try to run away, sighed and asked, "Do you know the story of the sandflea and the camel?"

"No," said the lion. "Tell it."

So the desert fox began:

"Once a camel rode on a sandflea from here to Sidi Ifni. When they came to a large waterhole, the camel said to the flea: 'You drink first to regain your strength so you can carry me on.'

"So the flea crouched at the edge of the waterhole and drank all the water down to the very last drop. The camel couldn't even wet his tongue. He became so weak that he died of thirst soon after his ride continued.

"Immediately the sandflea ate the camel. And ever since the flea has lived as a free animal in the desert and is beholden to no one."

"Not bad," roared the lion. "Now you lie better, jackal, if you can."

The jackal, who knew the lion had never seen the ocean, asked, "Have you ever heard the story of the people who died of thirst in the middle of a waterhole?"

"No," said the lion. "Tell it."

So the jackal began:

"There is one waterhole so big that one needs months to swim across it. It is called ocean. On this waterhole there swim iron houses that are called ships. On these ships peo-

THE LION THE JACKAL

ple ride from one edge of the waterhole to the other.

"Once there came a great wind that made such waves on the water that one ship with many people on it was unable to land and had to stay on the water for two weeks. The people died, one by one, because the water of the ocean is so salty that no one can drink it."

"Oho," roared the lion, "that is the craziest of all the tall tales I have ever heard." He laughed, roaring so loudly that a hyena a half day's flight away from him heard and was startled.

"All right, now let's see how you will do, gazelle!" roared the lion. "It had better be good or you'll be my dinner."

The gazelle, an experienced animal that had traveled far, hissed out of a corner of her mouth to the desert fox, "Sneak away while the lion is listening to my story." Then she asked the lion loudly if he knew why so many crows came to the desert in the beginning of the year.

"No," said the lion. "Tell me."

So now the gazelle began:

"In the North there is a land where it is bitter cold at the turn of the year. Wet flour falls from the sky, which is called snow. From this snow the children of the northland make men, whom they call snowmen.

"Later in the year, as it becomes warmer in the North, snow stops falling and the snowmen must melt. The snowmen know this, and they beg all crows to fly south and stop the sun from making the trip up North. For this the snowmen give the crows their long noses, which are delicious carrots.

"Actually the crows fly south to us in the desert every year, but they cannot stop the sun by their flight. So the snowmen melt every year, and the crows caw in the desert."

"For all the sand and desert wind!" roared the lion. "That is definitely the wildest of all the stories I have ever

THE CROW

THE SNOWMAN

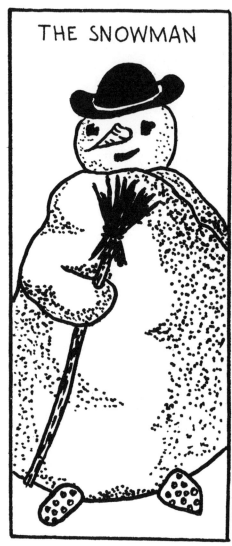

heard. Melting flourmen! Who has ever heard of such a thing?"

"Snowmen," corrected the gazelle.

"Snow or flour, well told is well told," said the lion. "And now I shall eat the desert fox. He was the poorest liar."

But as the lion looked around for the desert fox, he found that he was gone.

The lion, who was a good loser, laughed and said, "I tried to be clever, but the desert fox outwitted me. Farewell, and tell the desert fox that when I see him again no lie will save him."

Brahim, the trader, let the sleeves of his robe glide off his shoulders again, brewed some fresh tea from different herbs, and said, "When the Tuaregs hear this story, they really believe that the gazelle told the best of the lying stories. People who live in the desert do not believe in snow. Have another sip of tea."

Next week, Pauline, I'll have some tea
with Brahim again. Maybe he'll tell me a new
story. If it is not too long, I'll write it
down for you in the Sahara.

Since I don't know exactly when I'm flying
to Africa, I beg you not to send me anything
more, unless it's a letter. The rhymed composition is free, a bonus.

Say "Hello" to your family, the snowman,
and the crow, and stay winterly well, the
same way it is possible to stay summerly well.

Your Don Jaime

Don Jaime

PAULINE TO THE AUTHOR

*About stories that are half crazy
and half sensible,
silly Harry and country-folk*

Dear Don Jaime,

In this letter you will find a picture of me that you can take with you as a remembrance when you go to Africa. It is also a bonus, just like your rhymed composition for which I can hardly wait.

That the birzel looked different to you than it did in my drawing might, of course, be your fault. I'm sure I look different to you than I do to my brother, Klaus. Don't you think so?

I like the story told by your friend Brahim. It is half silly and I think that is the best kind of story. What do you think? The story and the weather make me look forward to spring. It is muddy outside. The poor snowman is dripping and has lost his nose. The crow no longer visits him. Well, such is

life, as my father says. (Or do you
suppose the crow has flown south with
the nose?)

Please be sure to write me from
Africa. If Brahim's new story is too
long, I will understand. You don't have
to write it down for me. You have already
sent me so many stories. Do you plan
to make another book from them? With
the poem at the end? Since you wrote
the stories for me, the title might be:
Pauline and the Animals. But, of course, I
leave that up to you. I don't want to
be pushy.

My family has finally stopped
bizeling, except for Harry. He has
become really silly. Maybe he would like
the story of Polly Plauz now. The farmer
Hartl liked it. He said Polly Plauz is

just good natured, like country-folk. That
is why she kept on carrying the trunks for
the dancers. Apparently everyone sees
something different in a story.

All good wishes from us for your trip
to Africa. I'll draw a picture of how
you will look there. If you'll throw the
poem into the mailbox, I'll be very happy!

Many good wishes from
your faithful Pauline.

me

you in the desert

THE AUTHOR TO PAULINE

*Contains wise thoughts
about anticipation and eternity
and the Legend of the Heavenly Snail*

Dear Pauline,

Thank you for your letter and the picture of
yourself. I will be going away tomorrow. But
before I leave I want to thank you for all you
have done for me: for sending me so many much-
needed items, and for giving me ideas for
stories. I've saved all of our letters, and I
hope they'll make a book. Your name will be
on the front page, and all the way through as
well. But I don't want to call it <u>Pauline
and the Animals.</u> Instead it will be called,
<u>Letters to Pauline.</u> (Just like in the draw-
ing here.)

I have finally finished the poem you
wanted. It tells of the problems the heavenly
snail has in delivering all the animals in
her house to the heavenly gate.

You might not want to show it to Miss Hirsch
or to the Most Reverend Mooshammer. It may
be better just to keep it between the two of us.
(If they should read it in the book, they
can't blame us; that's their own fault.)

It's nice to read that Harry is still
birzeling. Tell him that that makes me ve

LETTERS TO PAULINE

ha (very happy).

I am glad, too, that farmer Hartl liked the octopus story. I've always said he understands something about storytelling.

You are certainly welcome to the poem, or, if you prefer, the rhymed composition. I am copying it down for you with appropriate illustrations:

The Legend of the Heavenly Snail

Here with wonder and amazement
Hear the song of heavenly snail
Who among the fluffy cloudlets
Leaves a slow but steady trail.

On her back a giant snailhouse,
As she travels through the skies,
Where the animals are carried
Toward the door of paradise.

THE HEAVENLY SNAIL

But the snail she moves so slowly,
Though her house may throb and roar,
In a hundred years she's covered
But a foot or two, no more.

She moves ahead, this ark of heaven,
With her thousand whirring guests,
Who await an unknown moment,
A golden door, a place that's blessed.

There inside that crowded snailhouse
Those of hoof and those of wing
Speak of nothing as they journey
But the joys one day will bring.

At the very topmost lookout
Sits the eagle, proud and bold,
Who, unblinking, scans the distance
For a glorious glint of gold.

Under him are seven owls
Gazing at the Milky Way,

FRANCIS IN THE SNAILHOUSE

THE SEVEN OWLS

Hoping that the stars will tell them
Of the glad arrival day.

And down one level lower
A flock of bats shriek out a tune,
Thinking bats behind the gateway
Will pipe out an answer soon.

In the middle of this turmoil
Is Saint Francis, kind and good,
Writing in a heavenly log book
What the creatures say he should.

143

With their pointed ears alerted
Under him the lynxes wait
For the trembling sounds of harpists
Who may be playing at the gate.

There's a marmot one floor lower
In a limp and quiet heap.
He would like an endless journey
Just to sleep and sleep and sleep.

All the fish are at the bottom
There they swim, they're happy, gay;
Why, they wonder, are they going
To a fearsome judgement day?

It's open ears and eyes and mouths
As all the others do no more
Than await the day of glory
Await the opening of the door.

So the grand old snail keeps crawling
Thousand years on thousand years

THE GOLDEN DOOR

Through the endless clouds of heaven,
And who knows when glory nears?

Maybe we should all want to sit in the snail's house, for it may hold anticipation through all eternity. And anticipation is surely the better part of happiness. But we are still very much alive on our beautiful earth, you in Bavaria and I, as of tomorrow, in Africa. And of that we can be glad, for eternity can wait.

Stay happy, Pauline, in all your snow and slush. Look forward to spring and give my regards to your gigantic family!

> Your old friend,
> Don Jaime

P.S.: I'll write to you from Africa!
                              J.K.

Don Jaime